OLD MONEY,
NEW MONEY

OLD MONEY, NEW MONEY

Peter Sheridan

LARGE
PRINT

First published in 2000 by
New Island
This Large Print edition published
2010 by BBC Audiobooks by
arrangement with
New Island

ISBN 978 1 405 62296 7

British Library Cataloguing in Publication Data available

Printed and bound in Great Britain by
CPI Antony Rowe, Chippenham and Eastbourne

CHAPTER ONE

Hugh 'Redser' de Barra hated doing the paper round on his own. He delivered Catholic papers to the legion of Mary. It took him all around the North Wall. He went to houses along Seville place, where he lived. He delivered to people living in cottages along the canal. The flats in Sheriff Street were part of his round. He had customers in Brigid's Gardens and Laurence's Mansions. They were badly named—they had no gardens and no mansion. The papers took him over the bridge to the East Wall, too. In short, it took Redser to the four corners of the parish.

It was a long way to walk on your own. There was a saying he'd learned at school—'two shorten the road'. He'd learned it in Irish. *Gioraíonn beirt bóthair*. Redser was good at

Irish. His father came from Donegal, where it was still spoken. That's why they'd kept their Irish name, de Barra. Redser was christened Hugh after another Donegal man, Red Hugh O' Donnell. That was how he got the nickname Redser. He didn't have a single red hair anywhere on his body. It didn't matter because he liked his nickname. One thing Redser didn't like was doing the paper round on his own. They were supposed to deliver the papers in twos. His partner, Timothy Keegan, hadn't turned up. Redser hated the thought of walking all around the parish on his own.

He thought of calling around for Pancho. Christopher Nolan was Pancho's real name. One Christmas he got a sombrero from Santy. Somebody in Sheriff Street called him Pancho and the name stuck. Pancho was Redser's best friend but he hated anything to do with the Legion of Mary. Redser tried to get him to join several times. His sister, Catherine, became a member, but not Pancho. The problem was he didn't believe in God. He stopped believing in God the day Joseph Kavanagh was killed in Sheriff Street. He was run over by a coal lorry. His remains were splattered all over the cobblestones. The accident happened right opposite the shrine to the Little Flower. He was the second member of the family to die that year. His sister, Marcella, had drowned in the canal four months earlier. After Joseph was killed, Pancho declared that God was stupid. How else would he have let that happen? Everyone rounded on Pancho. It wasn't God's fault, they said. God never slept, everyone agreed. In that case he must be dead, Pancho concluded.

Redser knew that God was alive. There were too many churches for Him to be dead. Too many people saying prayers for Him not to exist.

He had to be out there somewhere. Anyhow, he didn't want to argue with Pancho about it. He wanted him for the company on that paper round. Redser knew that he would come back to his religion sooner or later. He was only thirteen after all. His birthday was the 11th of June. He was born Christopher Nolan in the Rotunda hospital. Redser knew this because he was born Hugh de Barra in the same hospital on the 10th of June. They were babies in the hospital together but Redser was a full day older than Pancho. Whenever they had an argument, Redser reminded his friend that he was older than him. This drove Pancho mad because Redser claimed he was wiser too.

Redser bounded into Brigid's No-Gardens. He was going to call on Pancho to keep him company. He could only say no, after all. Under his arm he had his papers—the *Catholic Standard*, the *Catholic Herald* and the *Universe*. They were papers full of God. They were full of someone Pancho claimed didn't exist. Redser skipped up the steps to the top balcony. On his arrival at Pancho's front door, he heard crying coming from inside. He peeped in through the window. Tommy Nolan, Pancho's father, was sitting at the table. In his hand he had a bottle of Jameson whiskey. He raised it to his lips and almost missed. He took a slug and offered it to Mrs Nolan. He mumbled something but it was impossible to make out the words. Mrs Nolan shook her head and cried, 'Have you any of the money left or have you drank it all?' Tommy Nolan brushed off her question with a wave of his hand.

Redser was surprised to see Pancho's father there. He had been missing for nearly three weeks. He was out on a bender. It wasn't an ordinary bender. It was a massive bender. An ordinary bender went on for two or three days. Maybe even a week. But this was a bender for the record books. Over two weeks and drinking every day. Not coming home. Not for food, not to change clothes, not to wash.

Pancho had gone looking for him in the pubs on the quays. He tried all his usual haunts—Liverpool Bar, Champions, Byrne's Pub and Coyle's Select Lounge. He'd been buying drink for half of Dublin, Pancho was told. But there was no sign of his da. Rumour had it that he'd gone over to the south side. That was a big move for a docker from North Wall. Pancho didn't have a clue where to start looking over there. So he came home and told his mother. All they could do was sit tight and wait for his return. Wait for the money to run out. Wait until he drank himself sober. Wait until he got sense. Whatever way they looked at it, all they could do was wait.

Now he was home, and he was far

from sober. Had Redser known, he wouldn't have called round. Pancho had always got mad when his father was drunk. Some men drank and got merry. Other men bought fish and chips and brought them home. Some men even threw their money away in a rush. Tommy Nolan wasn't like that. When he got drunk, he came home and started a row with his family. He picked on someone and blamed them for his drinking. If anyone answered him back, he got violent.

Redser looked in at the awful scene. Mrs Nolan crying and asking the same question over and over again, 'Have you got any of the money left?'

Catherine and her younger brother, Tommy Junior, sat in silence. They were afraid to move. Anything they did could provoke him to lash out. Above all else, they didn't want him lashing out at their mother.

Redser was struck by how bare it all was. The walls were bare and the table was bare. The presses were closed but Redser knew they were empty. There was no food in the house. It had a hungry look, a defeated look. Redser was helpless to do anything. He'd never gone a day hungry in his life. At worst, there was always bread and tea in his house. Or Marietta biscuits and jam. He hated Tommy Nolan for doing this to his family. Why couldn't he see that food was more important than drink? Why did he blame others when he was at fault?

As the eldest, Pancho always got the worst of it. He stood up to him, which only made things worse. He wasn't standing up to him now because he wasn't there. Maybe he was out looking for him and didn't know he'd come home. If he saw him drunk like this there was sure to be a fight. It was so predictable and so awful. Redser was angry that Pancho was trapped. He turned away from the window and walked along the balcony. He felt the weight of the papers under his arm. He hated having to deliver them. Yet, he was glad he wasn't Pancho. He blessed himself for his luck. He wondered was there anything he could do for his friend. He couldn't take his place, even if he wanted to. They could have swapped places at birth, but it was too late for that now. Fate was such a peculiar thing, Redser thought. They were born in the same hospital on almost the same day. They should have been friends from there on but they weren't. It was chance that had thrown them together. Nothing but pure chance.

CHAPTER TWO

Redser de Barra and Pancho Nolan on their first day in the big school.

They had known each other in the little school but they had sat in different rows. It was only when they went over to the Christian Brothers that things happened. They were put standing in a line against the wall. Their new teacher, Brother Armstrong, looked like a cheetah prowling over them. He had green, flashing eyes. He looked like a cat about to pounce on its prey. He called out a name and a boy put his hand up like a frightened mouse. He pointed to a desk and the mouse sat down. He consulted the roll book and picked out another name. That was how Pancho and Redser ended up sitting together like paired mice.

At eleven o'clock, Brother Armstrong let his charges go out into the playground. 'I'm glad I'm sitting beside you, Redser,' Pancho said, 'you've got brains.'

Redser was chuffed at the compliment. 'You've got brains too, Pancho,' he told him.

Pancho shook his head: 'I'm a dunce, Redser, you're sitting beside a dunce'.

Redser thought Pancho was joking. It was their first day in the big school and he was nervous. All the boys were nervous. Five more years ahead of them. Thousands of days with Brother Armstrong. It was too long to think about.

'My da was no good at school and neither am I,' Pancho confided, 'It runs in the family.

Redser had never met anyone like Pancho. All the other boys lied about how good they were at things. Dominic Foley claimed he was a genius at maths. Tom Bradley said he could run a mile in under three minutes. Myles Plummer was going to be the president of America when he got out of school. Pancho Nolan, on the other hand, admitted to being a dunce. Form that day, he became Redser's best friend. In fact, according to most things, they should have been enemies.

For a start they were opposite sides of the parish. Redser lived in a house and Pancho lived in flats. The two sides were like water and oil. They didn't mix. The men drank in different pubs and the women bought their messages in different shops. In the chapel, they knelt on opposite sides even though they prayed to the one God. There was a line dividing the parish in two. It was invisible but more real than if it had been painted by the corporation.

Redser and Pancho didn't recognise the invisible line. Pancho played in Redser's house and Redser played in Pancho's flat. Redser loved the view of Dublin from the balcony of the flats. More than that, he loved getting up onto the roof and inspecting the pigeon lofts. Nobody from the houses raced pigeons. Budgies in cages were all you'd see in the houses. The roofs of the flats were dotted with lofts. Pigeons flew down to the river and picked up grain in their beaks. After they'd stuffed themselves, they flew in formation to their lofts. It was a great thrill to watch them.

Pancho preferred Redser's house. He didn't care that much for pigeons. He loved the half-sized snooker table in Redser's front room. He had a great eye for potting balls. He knew how to play a screw shot and he could stun the ball, too. No one had thought him to do it—it came naturally to him. He glided around the table and stroked balls into the pockets. It was like poetry. Everyone loved to watch him but hated playing him. He was so good he didn't need to boast about it. 'It doesn't take brains to pot a few balls,' he'd say, 'It only takes a good eye.'

The only thing Pancho admitted to being good at was finding money. He was a genius at it. Walking along the street with him, he'd suddenly jump down. He'd come up with anything from a penny to fifty pence. It was like a sixth sense. It seemed he could smell money. On the footpaths, in gardens, down shores, there was nowhere safe for money to hide when Pancho was around. If he wasn't finding it, he was making it. Collecting empty jam jars, Guinness bottles, Harp bottles, cider bottles, he'd get a penny for each of them at the off-licence. His best money-making scheme was carrying cases.

One day he showed Redser the ropes. It was during the summer holidays. They hadn't the price of an ice pop between them. The sun was melting the tar on the streets. How they'd love to be going to Tara Street Baths. Or getting a bus out to

Dollymount Strand for the day. At Amiens Street railway station, Pancho placed Redser at one side of the steps. He stood on the opposite side. Together they waited for passengers. Passengers with cases. 'Remember, Redser, pick up a case and start to walk,' Pancho advised. 'Don't wait for them to say no.'

A woman with four cases struggled into view. She was pumping sweat. No wonder, considering the Aran sweater she was wearing. She had two small cases under her arms and two larger ones in her hands. Pancho pounced straight away. Redser followed his example. 'Can I carry your case, miss?' Pancho said as he took one from her. In seconds, the boys were heading up Talbot Street with the woman chasing behind.

'I'm going to the Gresham hotel,' she shouted after them.

'Just follow us so,' Pancho replied.

'Yeah, just follow us.' Redser echoed the command.

At the Gresham Hotel, the woman gave them a ten-shilling note. Pancho, for once, was speechless. Redser couldn't believe his eyes. A beautiful, crisp ten-shilling note. Bright orange, like the setting sun. They could do whatever they wanted now. The baths, the beach, the pictures—anything was possible. They went down to Matties, their favourite sweet shop, and stared in the window. The coconut bars looked appealing. So did the gob-stoppers. In the end they couldn't resist the lucky lumps. The chance of finding a thrupenny bit was too hard to resist.

They came outside too divide them up. 'One for you and one for me,' Pancho started off.

Redser put a hand out and stopped him. 'It's twenty each,' Redser said, 'twenty for you and twenty for me.'

Pancho looked at him and squinted. He was brutal at sums. Redser explained it to him but it was no good. Pancho put one in his mouth and started to suck. 'I'd love to have your brains, Redser,' he said. Redser knew it was useless to answer. Pancho had taught him more than any school could. Without Pancho there would be no lucky lumps to start with. There was no point telling him. If he said anything, Pancho would just find a way of putting himself down. So he said nothing and divided them up. Redser put one in his mouth and started to suck. He looked across at Pancho and saw he was biting into his. It was against the rules to bite lucky lumps. Pancho just couldn't wait to see what he'd find inside his. He had one in his mouth and nineteen more to go. He couldn't suck them all. It was torture. He had to find out as fast as he could what lay in store for him.

Pancho's luck didn't last. That night his father caught him in his bedroom sucking lucky lumps. At first, he accused Pancho of stealing them. Pancho said he found them on the street. When his father took off his docker's belt, he told him the truth.

'You made ten shillings carrying cases and you didn't bring it home here,' his father said in a rage. Pancho said he was sorry but it was too late. He got four lashings of the belt for being a selfish bastard. Four lashes for the lucky lumps that turned out to be unlucky after all.

CHAPTER THREE

Pancho sat on the floor of Benny Cunningham's pigeon loft. He sat with his back against the wire mesh. It was digging into him but he didn't care. He was sharpening a knife. He stroked the blade against a stone. Up and down he dragged it. Across and back, turning the blade. It made a rasping sound. The pigeons kept well away from him. They were afraid of their lives. Afraid they were going to be slaughtered. They had nothing to fear. It wasn't for them. The knife was being sharpened for human flesh. Pancho was going to use it on his father. He wasn't going to take any more slaps from his belt. He was to old for that now. He was thirteen and big enough to defend himself. He could defend his mother, too, if it came to it. He would defend anyone in the house from the drunken pig who called himself a father.

He held his finger against the blade. The skin almost parted. He liked the feeling of power it gave him. One tiny push and his finger would turn into the red sea. The blood was bubbling under the surface waiting to be released. He could make it flow or not flow. He could cut into the flesh and see the magic happen. It was only a split second away. If he did it, would the tension flow from his body too? He was so on edge thinking of what he might do to his father. Thinking of what his father had done to him. He didn't want to stab him. It was against nature. He couldn't control his thoughts. The pressure was too much. He could picture the knife in his father's chest. He could see the look of horror in his eyes. 'What have you done to me, son?' The words of his lips mixed with blood. He pulled the knife out and tried to get the moment back. He saw blood on his hands. Pancho looked down and saw that his finger was bleeding. The knife had pierced his flesh. It hadn't hurt. All he felt was relief. He'd cut himself but hadn't stabbed his father. He hadn't stabbed him yet. He wasn't sure if he wanted to. The cut in his finger made the bad thoughts go away.

Pancho struggled to his feet and opened the loft door. He came out onto the roof. In the distance he saw Redser with his papers under his arm. He called out to him and Redser looked around. It took him a minute to find where the voice had come from. Pancho waved his arms. As he did, a drop of blood fell from his finger and landed on his collar. Redser raised the *Universe* and waved it in a return gesture. Pancho put the knife in his pocket and got down from the roof. He joined Redser below. A minute later they headed off to the flats in Sheriff Street. Redser asked him if he'd join him on his paper round. Pancho wasted no time getting to the rub. 'I'm leaving home, Redser,' he declared, 'I'm going to head for England.'

Redser took it all with a grain of salt. He knew how his friend loved to be dramatic. 'Who's going to work your father's button if you go to England?' he asked.

Pancho sucked his finger but didn't answer. Redser's question shut him up. Tommy Nolan was a button man on the quay. It was one of the best jobs in Dublin. The button was a guarantee of work for life. Only a handful of dockers were button men. They were the chosen ones. A button passed down from father to son. It was Pancho's birthright. He wasn't going to walk away from his future by taking a boat to England.

As they passed the shrine to the Little Flower, Pancho nipped in. He knelt down at the lighting candles in front of the statue. Redser stood at the door. He could see Pancho's face in the polished collection box. He was going to kneel beside him and join him in a prayer. Then he remembered that Pancho was an atheist. With that, Pancho craned his arm under the brass box. He felt around, like a sweeping brush. Seconds later, he came up with a silver coin. It was a ten-pence piece. In fact, it was a florin. Since the new money had come in, the old florin was worth ten pence.

Pancho took the coin into McIntyre's chemist and bought a plaster strip. He had to get Miss McIntyre to cut a piece for him. Outside on the street, he sucked his finger and wiped it on his shirt. He handed the plaster to Redser and asked him to put it on.

Redser looked at the cut. 'You need some cream on that,' he advised.

Pancho looked at him and shook his head. 'It's a clean cut, now do what you're told,' he said.

Redser held the papers between his knees and took the plaster. 'Do you want me to give it a kiss?' he said.

Pancho said 'Yeah,' but in a way that meant 'I'll burst you if you do.'

Redser grabbed up his papers. He knew Pancho didn't want to go with him. He knew without asking. Pancho had the smell of money in his nostrils and there was no money in the Legion of Mary. 'My father sold his button,' Pancho announced. Redser was sure he'd misheard him. If not, it was a joke in very bad taste. 'My father sold his button and drank the money,' Pancho went on. 'I'm going to England if I don't kill him first.'

Redser couldn't get his head around the news. He didn't know a button could be cashed in. How could a man give away his future? And his son's future, too? What would make a man do that? It had to be insanity. An act of madness.

'How much did he get for it?' Redser asked.

'Two thousand pounds,' came the reply.

You could buy a house for two thousand pounds, Redser thought. He couldn't have spent two thousand pounds on a bender. Not even a three-week bender. 'How did he spend the money?' Redser asked.

'Half of Dublin's been drunk on it,' Pancho said through clenched teeth, 'and what he didn't drink he pissed away in the bookies.'

There were no words of comfort Redser could offer him. It was a tragedy, that was all. No stupid words could take away from it. It was madness, pure and simple. Tommy Nolan had drunk his button. He'd poured it down his gullet. Pancho's future was in ruins. 'What are you going to do?' Redser asked. It wasn't really a question because he knew the answer. Pancho had told him. He was going to England.

Pancho shrugged his shoulders. 'I might kill him, I suppose,' he said and laughed because it was true. 'I'll kill him and then go to England.'

Redser laughed, too, because he understood how his friend felt. Sometimes the only answer to madness was madness. Sometimes it was fun. Not when it turned into anger, though. Anger was a very powerful emotion. It was powerful enough to make you kill. Redser didn't want Pancho going to jail. 'Don't go home,' he said. 'Come on the paper round with me.'

Pancho didn't like the offer. 'I'd better make sure he's not breaking up the flat,' he said.

'I'll be home in an hour,' Redser countered.

'Come round for a game of snooker.' Pancho nodded his head but his mind was elsewhere. He turned on his heels and headed for the flats. Redser watched him before he set off to bring holy papers to the people of the parish.

CHAPTER FOUR

Redser delivered his papers but his heart wasn't in it. He was thinking of Pancho the whole time. His situation was hopeless. Redser tried to think of something positive. He couldn't find one thing. It was all grey and bleak like the Irish whether. There was nothing for Pancho to look forward to. He'd never tried at school because he didn't need to. He was going to be a docker when he grew up. He was going to inherit his father's button. What use was algebra for a Dublin docker? Or long division and subtraction? Pancho never tried because his future was assured. Now it was in ruins.

Redser turned left at the top of Guild Street. It brought him into the North Wall. The Liverpool boat was steaming down the Liffey. On the quayside, people were waving goodbye to their loved ones. It was mostly women. Crying for their men who had to leave. It would be Pancho's turn soon. Redser felt angry all of a sudden. He didn't want his friend to leave. He didn't want to stand at the quay wall and wave goodbye. He wanted him to stay in Dublin. They'd been together since their first day in the Christian Brothers. Pancho had taught him all the best things. He'd shown him how to carry cases. Taught him how to screw a snooker ball. Shown him how to find money in a shore. Brought him onto the roof to the pigeon lofts. He couldn't bear the thought of Pancho not being there. If Pancho left, he'd go with him. He couldn't let him go on his own. He was older than his friend and wiser. They would both have to go. It was the only solution.

It would be hard to leave school. Redser was good at school. Algebra, long division and subtraction were no problem to him. They might come in handy in England. He didn't know if they'd get him a job. He'd have to wait and see. Pancho had taught him to carry cases. Now they were going to carry their own cases into England.

It upset him to think of leaving the house. That was the hardest part. Leaving his ma and da. His brothers and sisters, too. Liam, Emer, Finn and Deirdre. The five de Barras.

They were very close. He didn't know how he'd tell them. Or if he'd tell them at all. It brought a lump to his throat thinking about it. He'd miss the snooker table, too, of course. And his own bed. He'd miss his pocket money on Fridays. He was giving up a lot. He would have no one to look after him. No one apart from Pancho. He thought about God. Somehow He seemed very absent. He didn't seem to be there. Maybe Pancho was right. Maybe He didn't exist.

What was he carrying under his arm if it wasn't the word of God? He still had half the delivery to do. He turned into New Wapping Street and headed for the East Wall witches. They were two elderly sisters living on their own. Molly and Sadie Kennedy were only ever known as the East Wall witches. The pathway from their gate to their hall door was completely overgrown. The porch was covered in cobwebs. The windows hadn't been washed in over fifty years. The net curtains were falling apart. They were nearly a hundred years old. So, too, were the sisters. Molly was ninety-two and Sadie was eighty-eight. Between them they'd lived for one-hundred-and-eighty-years. In that time they'd collected some blackheads. Their faces were held together by black dots. Their hands were caked in grime. The rest of them was covered. They each wore a black shawl, a grey blouse that had once been white, and a black skirt. Their size made them frightening. They were barely four feet tall. Their hair was in one clump. They looked like dolls that moved. They had a constant shake. Their hands shook, their heads shook, and when they spoke, their voices shook. They always looked like they were about to run out of air. It was creepy to stand beside them. It was more creepy than standing beside a witch.

One of the few people they answered their door to was Redser. He was a lifeline for them. When he knocked, Sadie would peep through the net curtains. Her head banged off the glass sometimes because of the shake. Molly would come to the door and pull back the two bolts. Then she'd stand on a stool and turn the Yale lock. Sometimes it took her ten minutes. All the while she'd say, 'Don't run away, I'm coming to you.' Some day Redser expected her to crumble to the floor from the effort.

Once the door was opened, he was brought in. They'd make a great ceremony of paying for their paper. Molly would fetch her purse and Sadie would fetch hers, too. It was always a great race to see who would get their money first. More than once the contents of one purse or the other were spilled on the floor. Redser would have to get down on his knees and pick up every coin. He was very careful to avoid the mouse droppings. They were everywhere. There wasn't a surface in the house that didn't have them. Their dining table was a mouse heaven. It was covered in food—bread, jam, butter, sugar and milk. Redser had seen mice run across it many times.

He pushed open the gate and walked down the path. When he reached the porch a cobweb got stuck in his mouth. He spat it out as best he could. He knocked on the door and waited. There was no sign of Sadie at the window. They would

miss him when he went to England—
he was sure of that. They'd miss him
when the weather turned cold. In
winter time Molly would bring out a
hatchet and an orange box. He'd
break it up and chop it into sticks for
her. She tried to do it herself
sometimes. It was terrifying to watch.
A miracle she never chopped off her
other hand. If Redser went away
she'd have to buy sticks instead.
There was nothing surer. He
knocked again. Something seemed
odd to him. He pushed against the
door and it moved. There was some
resistance but not much. He got the
door open enough for him to put his
head in. There, at the bottom of the
door, was a mound of black clothes.
The mound started to move. He
realised it was a person. In fact, it
was Molly. She started to moan. He
dropped his papers and bent down to
pick her up. Her forehead was
grazed and she started to shake. She
tried to talk but she wasn't able to.

She was in shock from her fall. She clung onto Redser and tried again to talk. The only word she could get out was 'upstairs'. Over and over again she forced out the word like it was her last breath. Redser assured her as best he could. 'It's all right, you're going to be all right,' he said.

They walked arm in arm into the dining room. Sadie was sitting at the table with the mice droppings. In front of her she had a shoe held up for protection. 'Upstairs,' she said 'they went upstairs.' Redser didn't know what she was talking about. He thought she meant the mice. 'The robbers went upstairs,' she said.

Molly squeezed his arm. He realised that they'd been broken into. Out of the blue, a door closed. They were still in the house, he thought. The blood drained from his body. He realised it was the hall door. He put Molly sitting on a chair. 'Are they still up there,' he asked nervously.

'They got the pension money and left,' she said.

Redser decided to have a look for himself. He went out to the hall and tip-toed up the stairs. Clothes were strewn all over the place. It was a total mess. In the front room, the chest of drawers had been pulled apart. The door of the wardrobe had been ripped off. It was lying against the window. Old letters and papers were everywhere. Handbags, too. There must have been a dozen of them in the room. They were ancient-looking things. He picked one up and opened it. It was full of rosary beads and old Mass cards. He picked up another. It was soft to touch, like silk. He squeezed the clasp open. Inside were perfectly cut pieces of paper. They'd been neatly arranged in the bag. He pulled one out and got the surprise of his life. It was a ten pound note. Old but new. It wasn't new money but it was crisp and clean. He looked back in the bag

and realised that every piece of
paper was a rectangle of money.
He'd never seen so much in all his
life. He ran his finger across it and it
felt like a fortune. He flicked the
notes and tried to count but his brain
couldn't calculate fast enough. He
snapped it closed and headed down
the stairs. He was delighted their
money was safe. He held the bag in
his hand like a trophy. He thought of
the crock of gold to be found at the
end of the rainbow. With each step
he took, a terrible idea began to
form. He would keep the money.
What good was it to anyone stuffed
in an old bag? It was fate that the
robbers had missed and he had
found it. It was meant to be his. Why
else would he have picked it off the
floor? Before he'd reached the
dining room, he'd made up his mind.
He walked out the hall door, went
into the garden and hid the bag
under a bush. He came back into
Molly and Sadie and told them he

was going to get the police.

CHAPTER FIVE

Redser couldn't sleep that night. He couldn't stop thinking about the money. Why had he done it? He wasn't a robber. He'd never stolen anything in his life. Apart from Mikado biscuits in Dooley's shop. And the odd penny from his ma's purse. Something had made him do it. An impulse, a force from outside himself. A voice inside his head told him it was his big chance. The same voice now kept him awake telling him he might get caught.

He wasn't the only one that couldn't sleep. Molly and Sadie were lying awake in the Mater hospital. They were brought there for observation. After he'd hidden the money, Redser had found a neighbour with a phone and dialled 999. A squad car arrived at the house followed by an unmarked car. Two detectives, Mullery and Mahon, came in and inspected the place. They interviewed Redser and asked him the same questions over and over again. Did he see the robbers? What did the look like? What time did he arrive on the scene? What did he do in the house? Why did he go upstairs? What did he see in the bedroom? Every time they got onto the bedroom, Redser could feel his heart pounding. It beat so loud he was sure they could hear it. At one point he thought Detective Mullery suspected something. He asked Redser had he ever gone upstairs in the house before? Redser hesitated before he said no and Mullery repeated the question. 'Think carefully before you answer,' he advised him. Redser thought his heart was going to come out through his mouth and onto the floor. The ambulance saved him. Once that familiar sound burst into the scene, attention swung to the sisters. They didn't want to leave their home but the ambulance men insisted. Molly and Sadie walked down their path wrapped in blankets. A crowd of neighbours had come out onto the street. They stared in hushed silence. Molly and Sadie stepped up into the back of the ambulance, bewildered by what was happening.

They couldn't sleep in the hospital. There was too much activity for sleep. Too much noise. Doctors and nurses came by every few minutes to examine them. Sadie loved the attention. Molly hated it and thought it would kill her. She wanted to get back to the safety of her own home, even though it wasn't safe. Sadie, on the other hand, loved the bed she was in. she loved the clean, white sheets. She couldn't remember the last time she was in a bed like it. It was so lovely, she couldn't sleep with the excitement of it.

Detectives Mullery and Mahon were awake, too. They were driving around the North Wall in their unmarked car. Slowly, they made their way along the quays and down Commons Street into Sheriff Street. They were looking for something but didn't know what it was. They were looking for clues, something from the house. A discarded purse. A handbag. A pension book. Anything that might pinpoint where the intruders came from. They drove past Laurence's Mansions and Brigid's Gardens. It was late and the flats were asleep. All the lights were out except for one. Detective Mahon noticed it and wondered what they were doing up.

*   *   *

Tommy Nolan was sitting at the kitchen table with his head in his hands. He was crying from the bottom of his stomach, torn apart with guilt. Mrs Nolan, sitting across from him, was crying too. She was wondering how they were going to manage. Pancho was looking at his father in disgust. He still had the knife in his pocket but he wasn't going to waste it on him. He was too pathetic to spend time in jail for. He'd take his chances in England. He'd go at the first opportunity.

Catherine brought in a fresh pot of tea and a plate of bread. It was all they had in the house. They only had it because Pancho had a found fifty-pence in his the turn-up of his father's trousers. Luckily Tommy was asleep at the time. Now he was awake and raging at the drink. 'I should never drink whiskey,' Tommy Nolan said, 'It's the whiskey makes me mad.' His words were full of genuine remorse.

'What good is that to us now?' his wife wanted to know. 'What are we going to do tomorrow?'

Catherine poured out the tea but her father couldn't drink it with the hangover. All he wanted was whiskey, all he could think of was whiskey, even though it had destroyed him. A glass of whiskey would at least stop the craving. That's how it was when he was in the DTs. He hadn't the energy to raise up his head. He spoke down to the floor. 'I'll never drink again,' he declared.

'We don't care about the drink,' Pancho answered him, 'What about the button?' 'It's gone and you can't get it back.'

Tommy Nolan sat up in the chair and pulled his hands from his face. He wiped his eyes with the backs of his hands. He gritted his teeth and stared at Pancho. 'I'll get that button back if it's the last thing I do on this earth,' he said.

For a moment, Pancho felt something other than hatred for his father. Tommy Nolan meant what he said. He was making a promise because he was really sorry. He knew he'd done wrong and there was no justifying it. Pancho recognised this but the good feeling towards his father didn't last long. He'd seen it all before. He'd promised to take the pledge. Promise to join the pioneers. Promise never to take off his belt. The flat was littered with broken promises from him. It was always tomorrow when everything would change. Tomorrow he'd go off in search of a cure. Something to stop the shakes. That was the reality. Getting back the button would be the last thing on his mind.

It was five o'clock in the morning. Redser hadn't slept a wink. Sleep hadn't even threatened. It had never happened to him before. He was so awake, he felt he would never sleep again. It was a heavy price to pay. Lying in bed awake throughout the night was awful. The bag of money was a serious robbery. He wondered how much it was. He tried to count it in his mind. It wasn't at all like counting sheep. It kept him awake.

He figured it was at least a thousand pounds. Maybe even twice that. He counted it in tens. He stopped at two hundred. He added a nought. It was a quick way of multiplying by ten. He was good at sums.

There might be enough to buy back the button for Pancho. That was why he'd stolen the money. He didn't know at the time, but God had put it in front of him. It was God that gave us temptation. That's how he tested our faith. He had no doubts any more: God existed. He'd put the bag his way and Redser had taken it. He'd hidden it under a bush. It wasn't really stealing. He'd taken it on Pancho's behalf which made it all right.

These thoughts helped to calm Redser after his questioning by the detectives. He was awake but he was calm. His heart was beating normally. He was at peace. What he'd done wasn't really a crime. Then he thought of the awful word.

The word that plunged him into despair. The word that made his heart beat inside his head. So much that he thought he might explode. The word that took over his entire being was 'fingerprints'. What he had left all over the bag in the bush. His fingerprints. The marks on the top of his fingers that made him different to everyone else in the world. Mullery and Mahon already suspected something him of. If they found the bag they'd find his fingerprints. He'd go to jail. What would he say to his ma and da? What would he say to the Legion of Mary? What would Molly and Sadie say to him then? His life was in ruins. All he could think of was dying in his sleep. Falling into a deep sleep and never waking up. But he couldn't even get to sleep, so how could he die? He was so awake, it hurt. He would never sleep again. He put his left hand out of the bed and felt the iron frame. It ran from the head to the bottom of the bed and supported the springs. It was hard against his touch. Hard and strong. He rubbed the tops of his fingers along its surface. It gave him a burning sensation. He didn't care about the pain. He kept the action. All he could think of was getting rid of his fingerprints. He rubbed and rubbed until he thought he'd done enough. Then he turned over in the bed and started on the right hand. He kept it up all night. By morning, the tips of his fingers were shiny and black. His fingerprints were gone. He got up to wash himself and thanked God he'd made them disappear into the iron on his bed.

CHAPTER SIX

Redser spilled out the whole story to Pancho the next day. He just started talking and didn't stop until it was all out. He was glad it wasn't a secret any more. He was glad to have someone to tell. He was glad to have a friend like Pancho.

Pancho didn't believe him. A bag full of money, all notes, no coins? Found in the bedroom of the East Wall witches? Now stashed under a bush in their garden? It didn't seem possible to him. He prided himself on knowing where money might be hiding. He'd never have suspected the witches' house. The witches' was the last place he'd have looked for treasure. He had seen them begging for money one day. He remembered because the older one had a hatchet in her hand. He thought it was an odd way to look for money. They hadn't a shilling and they were threatening people. He recounted the story for Redser by way of proof that they were paupers. He was hardly going to believe that they were nearly millionaires. 'Are you sure it wasn't fake money?' Pancho asked. Redser shook his head.

Redser was annoyed at the world and that included Pancho. He knew the sisters weren't witches. He hated Pancho referring to them as witches. He also knew that they never begged. Molly carried a hatchet when they needed firewood. She was looking for an orange box, not money. They had their own money and they had their dignity, too. Redser didn't need Pancho taking it away from them. Only that he was nervous he'd have taken his friend in a headlock and made him take it back. He'd have done anything only he was about to steal their money. It made him confused. He was edgy. It was down to not sleeping. He might never experience sleep again. It was a terrible price to pay. He didn't know whether he was coming or going.

They headed over the bridge and headed into New Wapping Street. Redser immediately wanted to turn back. There were two women on the path staring at the house. Two neighbours who feared for their lives and their safety. Bad news travels fast and they'd come to view the scene of the crime. 'Look straight ahead and keep walking,' Pancho advised. As they passed the front gate, Redser averted his eyes but he didn't have time to tell if the bag was still there. He and Pancho walked down to the river and messed about on the steps before heading home.

That night, under cover of darkness, they returned. Redser brought his school bag with him. He also brought some papers. They had it all worked out. They pushed open the front gate and walked up to the hall door. Redser bent down as if to pushed the *Catholic Standard* through the letterbox. Pancho had a good look around to make sure that the coast was clear. He gave the signal—two short whistles. Redser hopped into the garden. He pulled back some branches and there it was, exactly as he'd placed it. He opened his school bag and stuffed it in. He rejoined Pancho and the two boys sauntered off like they hadn't a care in the world.

They went to Pancho's house to count it. Tommy Nolan was in the kitchen with two men. They looked like they were from the Vincent de Paul. They wore suits and matching shoes and looked as if they had charity to offer. Tommy Nolan asked the boys to go into the bedroom. Catherine, Junior and the rest of the Nolan kids were in there being very quiet. 'What's up?' Pancho asked.

'Da is giving up the drink,' Junior answered.

Pancho looked to Catherine who nodded in agreement with her younger brother. 'Those men are from the AA,' Catherine said.

'What's the AA?' Pancho wanted to know.

'It's the Automobile Association,' Redser said.

'Why is he seeing them about the drink?' Pancho asked.

A knock came on the wall. It was Mrs Nolan from the other bedroom telling them to be quiet. Everybody quickly obeyed. It was no laughing matter if Tommy Nolan was giving up the drink. It was like the house was holding its breath. They would have to wait until the men left before they could let it out. Catherine broke the silence. 'They have something to do with alcoholics,' she whispered, 'and no one is supposed to know about it. It's top secret.'

Pancho left the flat followed by Redser. They got up on the roof and entered Billy Cunningham's pigeon loft. There was no light because Billy had removed the bulb. All they had was the light from the moon.

It filtered through the holes and the cracks. He boys sat on the floor opposite each other and put the school bag between them. Redser opened it and looked at the handbag. Pancho took it in his hands and held it. He touched it all over. He smelled it. He felt its weight. He threw it gently in the air and caught it again. 'If it's real money,' he said, 'there's over two thousand of it in that.'

Redser snapped it open. They started to count the money, just like they'd counted the lucky lumps. They were kids then. They were still kids, in a way, but it was an adult amount of money. Ten, twenty, thirty, they started and counted to one hundred. They made a pile and started again. The piles mounted up. When they'd finished, there were twenty-six piles and four spare notes. Redser did the multiplication in his

head. Pancho counted it. He didn't
stop counting until he got to two
thousand six hundred. The four
spare notes made it a grand total of
two thousand six hundred and forty
pounds. It was over two thousand,
just as Pancho had said. It was
enough to buy back the button with
money over.

Pancho was as excited as he'd ever
been. He loved money. He felt
comfortable around it. It agreed with
him. Redser, on the other hand, felt
ill. Now that he had it in front of
him, it filled him with terror. He felt
like getting sick. He could easily have
drowned the money in a sea of
vomit. He wanted Pancho to get the
button back but he wanted the
money out of his life. He felt about
the money the way Pancho felt about
his father's belt—it was going to
punish him. He could see the delight
on his friend's face. It was the same
as the day they shared the lucky
lumps. But this was very different.

This wasn't just about sucking a sweet for ten minutes. This was about the rest of his life. It could make him sad and keep Pancho smiling for millions of minutes to come.

Pancho waved his hands above the pile like a magician. 'Have you noticed anything?' he asked Redser. Redser hadn't. He pointed to the picture on one of the notes. It was a woman wearing a scarf. 'That's old money,' Pancho said. It was true. The notes were crisp and clean but it was old tender. There was new money now and the old money wasn't around as much. It took Pancho to notice it. He was waving his hands like he'd made the money appear from nowhere. Redser got afraid someone might walk in on them. He gathered up the piles and stuffed them in the bag.

Pancho suggested going to the chipper for a one and one, which was a ray and chips. Redser turned on him. 'We're not spending the money on food,' he said.

Pancho put his hands in the air in a gesture of surrender. 'It was only a suggestion, Redser, that's all,' he said.

Redser was in no mood for Pancho's crazy ideas. 'We're buying the button ands what's left we're giving back,' he said.

Pancho was horrified. 'You found that money,' he said, 'it's yours. Finders keepers, losers weepers.' Redser knew it wasn't that simple. He hadn't found it. He'd stolen it. He'd hidden it under a bush. It belonged to the sisters, Molly and Sadie, and nothing would ever change that. He told Pancho to find out who they had to pay down at the docks for the button. He headed for home with the bag under his arm and his nerves all twisted up. It was strange having so much money and not wanting to spend it.

The following night Pancho called

over for a game of snooker. It was quiet in Redser's house. His parents were off helping at the local credit union. His ma helped take the money in and his father gave out the loans. They'd been involved in the credit union ever since it started in the parish five years earlier. Redser had the run of the house on credit union nights. Sometimes he held snooker competitions. With his two older brothers and Pancho, they'd play doubles. Tonight it was just Pancho for obvious reasons. As soon as Redser had the balls set up, Pancho wanted to know where the money was. Redser asked him to find it. Pancho looked all around the room. He paused at the fireplace. Up the chimney maybe, but Redser's hands were clean with no sign of soot. He thought about under the snooker table—too easy to find, he figured. The radiogram was obvious but too obvious. He looked at the shutters on the windows. First right and then left. He walked over to the left-hand shutter and started to pull it out. There, in the space left behind it, was the handbag.

'How did you know it was there?' Redser asked.

'I could read it in your face. You gave it away when I looked at it,' Pancho said.

A knock came to the hall door. Redser pushed the shutter back into its slot to see who it was. There, standing on the front step, were detectives Mullery and Mahon. Redser's knees started knocking. 'It's the police,' he said 'What am I going to do?'

Pancho grabbed him by the shoulders and spoke into his face. 'You're going to open the door and sty calm, that's what you're going to do,' Pancho urged him.

Redser couldn't turn the lock with the seat on his hands. Finally, he got it open, just enough to look out. The two tall detectives smiled through the opening at him.

'We've got some news for you,' Mullery said.

'Can we come in?' Mahon asked.

Redser brought them in and introduced them to Pancho. He thought about his ma and da at the credit union. He'd be gone by the time they got back. He would never see them again except through prison bars. He looked at the floor and waited for them to take out the handcuffs. The stolen money had brought him nothing but bad luck and now his time was up.

'We caught the robbers,' Mullery said. 'They tried to buy a car with the stolen money.' Redser couldn't make out what he was talking about. Pancho, too, was taken aback by the news.

'The owner of the garage got suspicious when they tried to pay for the car in old money,' Mahon added, 'so he called us and we caught them red handed.' The detectives were smiling from ear to ear with their great success. They didn't know that standing less than two feet from where they were standing was more money from the house, a bag the robbers had overlooked.

'How much money did they get,' Redser asked.

'They got four and a half thousand pounds,' Mullery said, 'and we recovered another two thousand pounds later.'

Redser permitted himself a half-smile but Pancho was positively beaming. 'How did the witches have all that money?' Pancho asked. The two detectives looked at each other and frowned.

'He means the sisters,' Redser quickly added.

The detectives explained that they'd been saving their pensions for over twenty years. Every week they got the cash from the post office and stuffed it into bags. They put the notes away and survived on the small change. They'd been doing it for so long they didn't know how much money they had. They didn't even know where they'd put half of it. Worst of all, they didn't know what they were saving it for. A rainy day, something for their old age, someone to look after them. Whatever it was, they'd forgotten. The saving became an end in itself. They were sitting on a gold mine and living in poverty. Two furniture dealers had sweet-talked them at the door and they had let them in. They'd gone upstairs and found the bags of money. But they'd been caught by their own greed. They had tried to buy a fancy car and they were now safely behind bars.

'We called to the hospital to give the sisters the news and they asked to see you,' Mullery told him.

'I'd keep well in with them if I were you,' Mahon said in a fatherly tone.

They started to make their way to the front door. Redser let them out. Mullery turned to him on the steps and smiled. 'I thought you might be involved in the robbery,' he said, 'but I'm glad you're clean. Mind yourself, now.' He followed his partner to the unmarked car. Redser waited until they'd driven off before coming back in and closing the door.

CHAPTER SEVEN

Redser wasn't sure about God any more. He knew the devil was real. His paws were all over the stolen money. Normal money had a watermark. If you held it up to the light you could see it. The stolen money had the mark of Satan on it. His face was there if you dared to look. Redser had seen it once and that was enough. He looked at it and saw it smiling at him. It was a smile of invitation. 'You're welcome to my home,' it said. Redser felt like he was in hell—he didn't need an invitation. He couldn't sleep and couldn't control his thoughts. His brain felt like it was on fire. One moment he thought he'd committed the perfect robbery, the next moment he realised the money was useless. He could never cash it in. It was old tender. It was a complete give-away.

If he tried to spend it, it would bring the police straight to his door. Or Pancho's door. They'd both go to jail. What use was the button if they ended up in jail? The only good thing was that they might get a cell together. But ten years was a long time to be stuck in a cell, even with your best friend. It might be better for them to be separated. Redser couldn't stop his mind racing. If only he had the moment back. He cursed himself for what he'd done. He cursed himself for his thoughts. He cursed himself for losing God and finding Satan. There was no doubt, he was in hell.

He decided to visit the sisters. He trundled up the steps of the Mater Hospital, his guilt increasing all the way. He found St Teresa's ward. It was full of old women. Six beds on each side. There was no sign of Molly and Sadie. He stood at the door and looked up one side and then the other. An elderly lady waved at him. It could have been Sadie only she looked twenty years younger than her. He waved back and she beckoned him. He moved a couple of steps into the ward. She looked familiar but where did he know her from? Was she a relative? Then she realised it—it was Sadie minus the blackheads. Sadie with her hair washed and combed. It was a new Sadie, related to the old Sadie, but she was twenty years younger. In the bed beside her was Molly fast asleep. She looked like an angel without her hatchet.

Sadie woke up her sister and Molly got out of bed immediately to greet Redser. They had no living relatives so he was their first real visitor. The police had called and questioned them but Molly was not impressed.

'I don't like the police,' she confided in Redser.

'We don't trust them,' Sadie added.

With that, Molly took a bunch of keys from her locker and placed them in Redser's hand. She pointed out the hall-door key and the key to the mahogany bureau. She asked him to go to the house and open the bureau. On the right-hand side he would find their two pension books. On the left-hand side he would find a set of rosary beads. He was to bring them to the hospital and when they cashed their pensions they wouldn't see him stuck for a pound. 'We will look after you now, don't you fear,' Molly reassured him. Sadie said nothing but looked at him as if he had proposed marriage to her.

All the way home he felt for the keys to make sure it wasn't a dream. He knew what he was going to do. He didn't have to think about it—he could feel it in his gut. He saw an end to his nightmare and he was taking it. He stopped off at Seville Place and took the bag out from behind the shutter. He put it under his jacket and walked to New Wapping Street. He opened the hall door with the key and went straight to the bureau. Everything was as they'd described it. Pension books, rosary beads, letters, old purses and other documents. He placed the bag of money among the papers. It looked perfectly at home. It looked as if it had always been there. He left it and went to the neighbour's house. The same house he'd gone to the night of the robbery. He called the police station and asked for detectives Mullery and Mahon. They were out on patrol. He asked that they call to New Wapping Street. He went back to the house and waited for them.

Seven minutes later they arrived. Redser met them at the hall door and brought them through to the front room. He showed them the bureau and told them why he was there. He pointed out the pension books and the rosary. He put his hand on the bag and flicked it open. The two detectives stared at the contents. They were amazed. 'I wonder how much is there?' Mullery asked innocently. Redser came so close to blurting out the answer—it wasn't funny. He had to strangle the words and turn it into a cough.

Mahon put his hand into the bag and pulled out the wad of notes. 'We won't know how much is here by just looking at it,' he said. They sat on the musty armchairs and counted it onto the floor. Mullery made bundles of five hundred at a time. Mahon checked the bundles to make sure his colleague was right. As the hundreds turned into thousands, Mullery looked over at Redser. 'I bet you never saw that much money in all your life,' he said. Redser put on what he thought was his best look of disbelief. He kept it up to the point when he thought he might be overdoing it. They came to an end of the counting. Mahon took a piece of paper from his pocket and wrote down the amount. He handed

Redser a pen and asked him to witness it. He was about to sign his name when he looked at the amount. Two-thousand-five-hundred-and-forty, it read. They were under by a hundred pounds. He wondered whose pocket it had gone into. Or maybe they would split it. He decided to say nothing. He signed his name. Beside it, the detectives signed theirs.

They gave him a lift in the unmarked car back across the bridge. They pulled up outside his front door. Pancho was sitting on the steps waiting for him. The detectives praised him for his honesty. He made no comment.

'You weren't tempted to steal it, were you?' Mullery asked.

Redser looked him straight in the eye. 'Yeah, it did cross my mind,' he said.

Mullery nodded, satisfied with the answer.

'You're only human,' Mahon

added, 'sure we're all only human.'

Redser got out of the car and they drove off. Pancho looked at him as much as to say, 'Please explain.' Redser was in no mood for explanations. He wanted to sleep on the events of the day. So much had happened recently. Things that had kept him awake. For the first in ages he knew that sleep awaited him. It was the best feeling he'd had in months, years even. He'd bought back sleep by returning the money and he didn't care. He was at peace with himself and he wasn't going to let Pancho take it away from him.

He invited his friend in for a game of snooker. To his surprise, Pancho declined. 'Guess who's in there talking to your da?' he asked. Redser had no idea. He walked up the steps and leaned over the railings. There, in the front room of his house, sat Tommy Nolan and his father. They were in deep conversation. Redser was very surprised. Tommy Nolan kept rigidly to the Sheriff Street side of the parish. It was his first time in one of the houses. His first time crossing the invisible line.

'He's going to join the credit union,' Pancho said. 'He wants to get a loan to buy back the button.' Pancho laughed when he said it. It was a knowing laugh. Redser laughed, too. He laughed because it seemed like the best idea he'd ever heard. It was the perfect outcome to the robbery. In the end, he laughed because it was good just to laugh. Pancho got annoyed with him and that made Redser laugh until he cried. Pancho grabbed him in a headlock and wrestled him to the ground. 'What are you laughing at?' he demanded. 'Tell me what's so funny.' Redser tried to tell him but he laughed every time he opened his mouth. They lay there on the ground and everyone thought they were fighting until they heard the laughter. It just went on and on.

People in the houses heard it and people in the flats, too. It was that kind or laughter. It seemed like it would never stop.